Where you go ...
I go.

PaRragon

Bath • New York • Cologne • Melbourne • Delhi
Hong Kong • Shenzhen • Singapore • Amsterdam

The sun comes up and smiles on us
And starts to warm the early day.

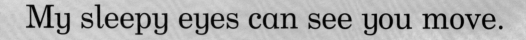

My sleepy eyes can see you move.

Where you go ... I go.

Then out we dash, to leap and play
And scramble in the morning sun.

You push some leaves
aside for me ...

(Hey Mom! Hey, look!
Guess who's a tree?!)

Let's go have fun, and mess about.

When you play ...
I play.

(Oh no!)

The skies turn gray,
It starts to rain,
And you just want to
keep me dry ...

(Thanks Mom!)

I run and shelter under you.
Where you are ... I am.

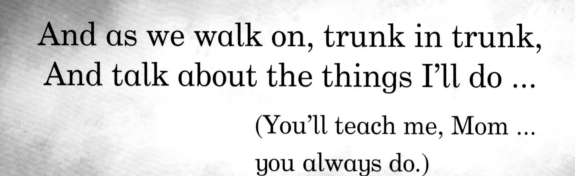

And as we walk on, trunk in trunk,
And talk about the things I'll do ...

(You'll teach me, Mom ...
you always do.)

You tell me just
how much you care,

("I love you Mom," I sing to you!)

What you love ... I love.

Then when it's time to scrub me clean,
We'll splish and splosh and splash about.

You wash away my bathtime fears,

(Just don't forget behind my ears!)

When you smile ... I smile.

And when the day has reached its end
And both of us are getting tired,

I'll snuggle up and feel your warmth.

When you sleep ... I sleep.

Beth Shoshan never thought she'd become a writer. Then one day she was challenged to write a children's book and the result was so good she's been writing ever since! She has written over 30 titles and is one of the most successful children's authors of the last few years.

Petra Brown has been a children's book illustrator since 2006 when her first picture book *If Big can ... I can* was shortlisted for the UK Booktrust Early Years Awards. Petra loves drawing animals full of character and personality.

This edition published by Parragon Books Ltd in 2015 and distributed by

Parragon Inc.
440 Park Avenue South, 13th Floor
New York, NY 10016
www.parragon.com

ISBN 978-1-4723-5923-0

Printed in China